That's My Best Friend

An Erotic Short Series

Dyphia Blount

Copyright © 2017 Dyphia L. Blount

All rights reserved.

ISBN: **10: 1976517427**
ISBN-**13: 978-1976517426**

Thank you all for your support in advance. Please don't forget to leave your reviews for a chance to win prizes for each release!

PROLOGUE

It was all good just a week ago...

Have you ever heard the term, "Y'all been hanging around one another so long that you're starting to look alike?" Well, I have. In fact, when Sasha and I go out, we hear that we look like twins. It's a turn on for us, and sometimes we end up acting out the part just for fun. We've shared everything from lipstick to underwear, and I knew that it was only a matter of time when we decided to share a man. We've always flirted with some of the same dudes and even discussed taking them home with the both of us, but if or whenever one of us was feeling him in a 'relationship' type way, the other fell back and let it run its course. We've never slept with one another; not even a friendly type kiss, yet we loved each other beyond what words could explain. We've gone through everything together; becoming a woman, our first love and lost, and even our first sexual experiences where one of us was in the closet filming.

Although we both looked and acted like one another, we were very different in our career paths as well as relationship views. Sasha was wild, outgoing, very free-spirited, confident and conceited, and high maintenance. I, on the other hand, am subtle, laid back, confident, and a hopeless romantic. I believe in happily ever after's and growing old together. Sasha has always expressed her feelings as though she was fine being alone, friends with benefits, or even a side-chick. You could say, I was looking for love and she was running away from it. If we both made time for one another when we did our separate things, we were good. But things took a turn for the worse about a week ago when we met Jermaine Spartan, but his friends *called* him Jay!

Sasha

Last Saturday night:

Mecca caressed her hardened nipples with sheer delight from the lashing of my tongue against her protruding clit! Her messy hair stroked the pillow connected by tears of ecstasy as she tossed her head left to right trying to understand how her best friend knew her hot spots. Her body was convulsing like beats to a drum as her hind-side lifted abruptly off the bed. I flicked my cotton soft lollipop licker on the hood of Mecca's love cave! When she heard the slurping of her juices mixed with my extensive sucking move, she lost her mind and grabbed two fist locks of my silky, long mane. I pressed my entire face against the bald bear and allowed my tongue to swim around in her forbidden fruit while my upper lips kissed her lower lips. When Mecca began to pant, and beg with her rotating hips and moan-filled mouth, I knew I'd mastered the technique, and the only thing left to do was bring it in for a home run!

I took my index finger and gently slid it into Mecca's perfectly plump ass while my other hand gripped her breast. Mecca's legs uncontrollably shook as if lightning struck her. Right on cue, she began to praise my name as if she was at the pulpit. Once her juices exploded, I slurped them up like a buttermilk biscuit swimming in hot, thick gravy. Mecca couldn't believe how good her best friend was at pleasing the box as I smiled to myself, quietly boasting of my immaculate, head giving skills! She'd taught me everything about teasing and pleasing her, and I'd planned on experiencing that magic every chance I got!

But...Mecca spoiled the moment when she said, "Girl, you good?"

I immediately snapped out of my trance and tried to steer the conversation away from the lustful thoughts I'd had for my friend I don't know how many times this week.

Mecca

"Girl, I'm going to kill them with this skimpy red dress and its slit down the front and the leg." Sasha boasted. With her breast and caramel-colored thighs, she was guaranteed to eat up every slit in that dress.

"I'm going with this elegant little black number. It's off the shoulder on the right, and a small slit in the back that accents my butt." I replied; looking at myself in the mirror, and feeling pleased with my selection.

I have a slender, but nice build, but I wasn't voluptuous like my best friend. I'm used to Sasha getting most of the attention whenever we go out, but it doesn't bother me because she always made sure we had a drink all night and never had to reach in our clutches. I adore her personality and sometimes wish I had her charisma. Don't get me wrong, I get plenty of attention, but I didn't demand it like Sasha, and that's where we were different.

We both decided to work the club that night and run some game. We wore our hair and makeup the same; in a Chinese bun, and accessories to match our dresses and one another. We were on the prowl tonight looking for a victim to participate in the one fantasy we've both had since we started having sex: a threesome. After watching one another's first encounter, we both decided that we wanted to bless somebody's son with both of our talents: where she lacked, I triumphed and vice versa. We promised that the first time we both were single and horny, we would go for it and that night was the night.

We couldn't even get into our parking space good with guys approaching the car trying to holler at us. The guys at "The Alley" were so desperate and thirsty. It was an immediate turn-off, and even if we saw them again in the club and they wanted to buy us drinks, we turned them down. They didn't play a fair game, and we liked men that matched our confidence. The type of men that weren't afraid of a little competition and managed to get our attention in a room full of eligible men were sexy to us. I know I speak for 'us' a lot, but what do you expect; we were best friends.

Once we got inside and settled at the bar, the games began. "Are Y'all twins? Sisters?" "Oh my God, I'm in Heaven, and God has blessed me with two angels." So many different, lame attempts that it started to be annoying after a while; for me, at least. I excused myself from maybe three drinks and twice as many men and headed to the restroom alone.

"I'll be right back," I mouthed to Sasha because the music was blasting Panda through the walls.

"I can go," she started to excuse herself as well, but I stopped her.

"I'm good babe. I see a little something, something that I may take home with us tonight." I nodded toward the ladies' room.

She squinted her eyes as if checking to see who I was talking about, but the sexy, chocolate man beside her whispered something in her ear that took her attention off me, and I was cool with that. I slid off my bar stool and started my journey over to the other side of the club. I said journey because just getting to the bathroom, passing a bunch of hungry, aggressive, and overbearing men was a task within itself. I didn't need any esteem boosters tonight, so I decided to head to the other side where I could at least breathe and make it to the bathroom with only one or two interruptions.

As soon as I hit the 'in-between' section, where you pay and check your coats, it felt like another world. I managed to get to the other side with only one hand-grab. Aliyah's "I Don't Wanna" was blasting from the speakers, but not too loud to hear yourself talk like the other side. Quite a few couples were on the dance floor, grinding and doing too much, while others were just mingling or at the semi-packed bar. The air was even different on that side. I could take several deep breaths and not feel like I was choking off cologne or covered up funk. I slowly walked to the bathroom to check my hair and makeup, and there he was...

"Shauna! Are you okay?" he seemed desperate.

I figured he'd fucked up and pissed Shauna off so; I laughed on the inside. Dudes were always flirting with other chicks and looking dumb while being all apologetic after getting caught.

"Excuse me," I looked him in the eye so he could move away from the door and allow me to enter.

"My bad Ma! I'm sorry, but can you do me a favor gorgeous?"

"Depends on what the favor is hon!" I locked eyes with him. He was gorgeous! He was talking, but I couldn't see past his full, chocolate lips. He was medium build and about six foot tall. His smooth chocolate skin was flawless, and his clean-cut hair dripped in waves. And he smelled delicious.

"Hellloooo!" his deep-toned voice rang out.

"I'm so sorry hon, what were you saying again?" I felt embarrassed.

He smirked and repeated himself, "My sister, Shauna just ran in there crying, and I just want to make sure she's okay. Would you mind checking on her for me?" he looked pitiful.

"Oh, of course, I will," I assured him before heading inside with him holding the door open for me.

"I'm Jermaine, but you can call me Jay…that's what my friends call me." He smiled and displayed the whitest teeth I'd ever seen.

I just stood there grinning like a Cheshire cat, forgetting that this was an introduction and that I should give him my name as well.

"Hi, I'm Ashamecca, but my friends call me Mecca!" I held out my hand for a quick shake.

He grabbed my hand and kissed it. "Pleasure to meet you, Miss Mecca. I truly appreciate this." He seemed to be sincere.

He pushed open the door a bit more to the ladies' room and nodded to remind me of my mission. Either he was a gentleman or eager for me to get in there and check on his sister, but it was cute nonetheless. I didn't have to pee anyway so why not help a sister out.

It wasn't hard to figure out where Shauna was because she was sobbing heavily in one of the stalls.

"Uhh Shauna, I'm Mecca! Your brother asked me to check on you." I pleaded by the stall door.

"Tell him to go away and find some fast ass chick to take home. It's his fault for bringing me here anyway." She yelled out.

"Honey, can you please come on out and let's talk about it?"

"I'm sorry, but I don't know you like that to talk to you about my business." She expressed between out loud cries.

"I know, but I'm just trying to help doll face!"

Slowly, the door opened, and Shauna walked out with her face covered with tissue to mask her tears and messy makeup. I immediately grabbed and hugged her which I was sure she wasn't expecting, but she embraced the hug and cried even harder.

My heart melted for her and I didn't even know what was wrong. We just stood there hugging for a few minutes while she composed herself well enough to get her words out. We were interrupted by Jay's heavenly voice calling out again, "Is everything ok in there?"

"Yes! We're good," I assured him. "We'll be out in a minute Luv!"

I heard a sigh of relief as the door closed.

"How do you know Jay?" Shauna asked between sniffles.

"Uh…I don't know him. He stopped me when I was coming in here and asked me to check on you. He seems to be worried about you, and I thought it was sweet."

"He *is* a sweetheart. He's my overprotective baby brother, and tonight was just way too much for me to handle. He'd been telling me to come out here to the Alley and put all the lies or truths to rest, and I guess I didn't want to know the truth." She backed away from me and looked in the mirror at herself.

"I mean, I know he has my best interest at heart, but damn."

I just stood there listening although a mountain of questions clouded my mind.

"My man came here every Saturday night and said he just wanted to hang with his homies, but my friends and some haters always came back with stories about his infidelities. I guess I felt like they weren't real if I didn't see them with my own eyes. Love is truly blind ya know?"

"Yeah, I know honey," I rubbed her back gently. "Some men are just careless with their actions. They never think of who they're hurting until it's too late." I started thinking about my last relationship for a moment.

"You mean to tell me that someone as gorgeous as you have men problems?" she turned her attention to me.

"Girl, looks don't make a happy relationship, people do. I was happy, but he wasn't. He felt like my best friend was too involved in our relationship and I wasn't going to diss my girl for no man, period." I shrugged my shoulders.

"Sounds like you're a good friend, ah…" she tried to recall my name.

"Mecca! Call me Mecca!" I smiled with embarrassment that we'd been sharing everything but names.

We both laughed and continued the conversation.

"As I was saying, your friends are very lucky to have you, Mecca. You seem to have your stuff all the way together. I wish I had friends like you. The females I deal with are like frienemies. Sometimes it's hard to tell if they're for me or against me, so I just stay in my lane and mind my business. That somehow works for me."

"I certainly understand. My best friend, Sasha, and I usually don't let anyone in our circle because females are so sneaky and funny acting."

"Hell, I thought it was all good on my part as long as I had my bae. We've been together for only three months, and he was all I needed until now. I just saw him leaving with some skanky looking whore. He didn't even see me. I'm not about drama, so I didn't even let him know that I saw him. Jay had been trying to get me to come here and confirm the speculations for myself for weeks. I guess I should be happy that I saw for myself, but it hurts way more than words could say." She shook her head.

"Well, at least you know and knowing is half the battle. Would you like to join Sasha and I for a drink to take your mind off things?"

"Really?" she seemed surprised.

"Sure, come on." I grabbed her by the hand, stole one more glance over in the mirror, and led her out of that awful smelling restroom.

I thought for sure that Jay would be hanging by the door like a hound dog, but he'd taken a seat at the bar and seemed to be just enjoying the music. He spotted us walking his way, and a wide smile formed on his handsome face. He stood up, motioning for us to sit next to him.

Sasha

Carl was looking and smelling good, and his choice of words had me ready to drop it like it was hot right on top of the bar, but I was worried about Mecca. She'd left over twenty minutes ago, and every time I glanced over to the ladies' room, there wasn't any sign of her. I remembered how much she hated using the bathrooms on this side of the club and figured she must've gone over to the other side.

"Hey baby," I turned to face Carl, and whispered in his ear, "Let me go find my bestie real quick and we'll be right back to take you home."

The look on his face said it all. He was shocked at my forwardness, but he wasn't disappointed. I saw a gleam come over his fine ass face as he parted his coochie-eating lips to respond…

"Uhhh, ok baby, whatever you want. You need me to go with you and protect Y'all from these busters?" he was ready to go suddenly.

"Naw, Suga. I got this. You just keep it warm for us and don't move because I'm only gonna look here for you once and if you're gone, it will be your loss." I smiled, licked the rim of his ear, and dismounted myself from the bar stool.

I've always been a straight shooter. I don't have time to play with these guys out here. They serve many purposes for me, but tonight I just needed Carl to serve one...The middleman! I needed him just to be the bridge that finally connects Mecca and me sexually. After tonight, she won't be looking nor wanting another dud-ass-dude. I was always attracted to both women and men, and my best friend never judged me on that or acted funny about it. I've been trying to sex her down for what seemed like forever but didn't know how to approach the subject or task.

I sashayed over to the other side, ignoring the whistles, stares, and attempts to grab my arm. I wasn't friendly like Mecca when it came to these dudes. If they dared to touch me, they got a rude awaking. If they didn't get the picture by me snatching away, a tongue lashing was soon to follow. She was just the opposite of me in many ways, and that's what I loved about her. She was so nice and social. She would just smile at a guy and let him waste her time before she snatched away from them like me. I was a Pitbull, and she was a Yorkie. I went after what I wanted, and she waited on prince charming to rescue her from her horrible castle. I was the alpha, and she was the beta which made for a perfect balance in our friendship.

I knew I was going to have to save her from some lame who was probably talking her head off and she would be sitting there smiling and trying not to be rude, but boy was I wrong. I saw her and another chic walking from the bathroom together, smiling and conversing when a rush of emotions took over me. I felt jealous. It was weird. I wanted...No, I needed to know who this chic was that MY friend was cackling with and entertaining.

I walked right up to them and stopped them in their tracks, "Uhhh, Harpo... Who dis woman?" I cocked my head.

The mystery woman laughed at me, but Mecca didn't. She knew I was dead serious and she tried to break the ice by dropping ole girl's hand and hooking her arm between mine that was placed on my hip, dragging me to the bar where Mr. Wonderful was standing. He was gorgeous. I didn't forget about Miss cheery on the other side of my friend, but he sure was a dick-straction that I was more than ready to get to know. Hell, he made Carl look like a school-boy. He was dressed quite spiffy; rocking a tailored ensemble, Rolex, and cufflinks. Can you say $$$??? He had it all, and I was ready to taste him with or without Mecca!

"Well, well, well. Who is this tall drink of hot chocolate?" I asked as I dropped Mecca's arm and locked arms with the cutie pie.

Love In This Club, Pt 2 by Usher came on, and I saw people headed to the dance floor to bump and grind. I glanced over at Mecca and her new friend and decided I wouldn't act up just yet. Once I feel her out, I will know if she's a threat or not. Until then, I wanted to grind on Mr. Awesome, so I grabbed his hand and pulled him onto the dance floor. The look on his face was priceless, but he didn't turn me down. I looked back at Mecca and ole girl, and their mouths we hung open with disbelief. I knew the conversation between them would be about me for the entire song, but I didn't care. We had a purpose tonight, and I wasn't going to steer away from it. I needed to talk this one up on the threesome of his life.

"Ummm, now that I've got you all alone, I can say what I want to say!" I hissed in his ear; holding him close to me.

"Oh yeah? And what is it that you need to say?" he questioned, putting a little swag on his slow drag.

"Uhhh just that you're the finest man I've seen in here tonight and I want to extend an offer to you that you can't turn down?" I switched my hips hard up against his manhood.

"But, I don't even know you." He whispered back.

"You know enough. You're cool with the other participant, and I'm sure she'll be good with it too." I turned around so he could grind on my ass.

"Soooo...you're telling me that Mecca is cool with having a threesome with a total stranger." He seemed baffled.

"Mecca is cool with whatever I say. Now, all you have to do is say the word, and we can be on our way." I bent over in front of him and bounced on it.

He pulled me back up and spun me around to face him, "You're cute...and so is Mecca, but that's not my cup of tea." He smiled.

"Then what is your cup of tea? Just call me Lipton!" I smiled back.

"I'm a coffee-type man myself. No disrespect to you." He eyeballed Mecca.

"Oh! I see. Well, what's her's is mine, and what's mine is her's. It's a two-for-one deal or no deal." I threatened, still smiling at his face.

"Then it looks like there won't be any love in or after this club after all!" he removed his manly hands from the nape of my back and walked back to the bar.

I was hot! No man ever turned me down or left me hanging. Who the fuck did he think he was, Jay-Z? It was time for me to grab what, I mean who I came for and bounce. I swiftly walked back to the bar and got in between Mecca and the 'side chick' and told her I was ready to go.

"Uhhh Mecca, Let's go!" I demanded.

"Damn Sasha. Why you gotta be all rude and whatnot?" she was puzzled.

"I'm not rude honey. We just got stuff to do, and this is a waste of time." I started to get irritated and put my hand on my hip to let her know I meant business.

She looked over at her soon to be ex-friends and apologized, "Hey guys, I'm sorry, but she's my ride." She tried to excuse herself before I made a scene.

"I can give you a ride," Shauna offered all chipper and shit. "Hell, Jay can even take you home." She looked over at Jay as he nodded yes.

"Fine! Stay your ass here with strangers then." I dropped her hand and hauled ass back to the other side where I'd left a very willing participant.

I knew something was going to fuck up the whole evening. I can't stand other muthafuckas all up in my business with my friend. I wasn't going to leave her there, and she knew that, but that wasn't the point. I was going to tell her ass about herself as soon as we got alone again. As I headed to the other side, I peeped Carl talking to a hottie and started to turn around and leave, but I felt like pulling rank tonight. Shit, I needed the ego booster after that ordeal a minute ago.

I didn't even have to say a word. Carl was looking around for me and spotted me coming. I heard him giving ole girl the boot as I approached, "Ummm, there's my girl, and I think she's ready to go." He nodded my way.

She looked away for two seconds to see who he was talking about, but by the time she turned back around to say something to him, he was hugging up on me. That's what the fuck I was talking about. *"Bow down bitches…the Queen is here."* I thought to myself. I could see him being an option after tonight; that is if the sex is good.

"Hey, baby. There's been a change in plans." I sniffed him to make sure no hoes were all over him while I was gone.

"Wait! What? Why?" he got upset.

"Calm down young man. Not like that!" I laughed. "My friend is a little pre-occupied right now, plus after thinking about it, I want you all to myself." I grabbed his penis and winked.

"You tryna get out of here then?" he was anxious.

"Let's go then!" Fuck it. I was horny and tired of this whack ass club for one night.

I was going to get me some head, maybe give a little head, and come back in after I send him on his way to wait for this pussy at his house. I wasn't going to miss out on that big piece of meat playing around with Mecca tonight. I let Carl lead the way to his car while all the other dudes that tried to holla at me that night looked on with jealousy.

Shauna

I couldn't believe the balls in Mecca's friend. First, she walked up to us all arrogant and shit, then she grabbed my brother's hand and practically yanked him on the dance floor. I don't even know how she and Mecca were friends; they were different, although it seemed they tried their best to look alike tonight.

"Damn Mecca! Your friend is a damn trip!" I shook my head.

"She's not that bad. She's just being Sasha." She defended her friend.

"And what the hell does that mean?" I was confused.

"It means, she's outgoing." She got on the defense. I could tell by the way she wrinkled her face, so I tried to ease her discomfort.

"I'm sorry Mecca. I didn't mean anything by it. It just caught me off guard the way she grabbed Jay and started doing her nasty little dance on him when he clearly has eyes for you." I softened my voice.

"Yeah, that's my best friend. She likes to play games and stuff. She didn't mean anything by it. Plus, she didn't know that Jay has eyes for me; hell, I didn't even know." She let her guard back down.

"So, that's what *Y'all* do all the time?" I interrogated her.

"Ohhh nooo. Not me. I go along with Sasha sometimes because it's fun. You just have to get to know Sasha. She's a good person who just likes to have fun." She smiled.

"Well, I don't know how you didn't know that Jay was feeling you. It was written all over his face. Didn't you see how big he smiled when we came out of the bathroom or were you wearing blinders?" I joked.

"Girl, I thought he was just happy that I got you out of the bathroom." She was naïve.

"Well, I know my big brother, and that look wasn't for me. His whole body language changed when he saw you and the last time I saw him look at a woman like that; he was ready to pop the big question to his ex, Cori." I started to fill her in on the details but noticed a strange look on Jay's face when Sasha bent her ass over in front of him.

"Oh wow! What happened?" she questioned with concern gracing her face.

"Never mind that, I will fill you in later. Hand me your phone so that I can put me and Jay's number in it, and we all can get up some other time because I don't think your friend cares too much for me." Before she could say anything, I grabbed her phone, added us as contacts, and dialed my number so I would have hers as well.

"How do you know Jermaine wants me to have his number? He looks like he might be interested in Sasha if you ask me?" she looked sad.

"Because he's *my* brother. That's how I know! He is just a nice guy and didn't want to embarrass your friend. He doesn't like fast in the ass women. No disrespect to your friend." I wasn't going to let her bow down to her whorish little friend this time.

I could tell who called all the shots in their friendship. That Sasha was a piece of work and Mecca deserved better than that. She could have at least asked if she was interested in Jay before she threw herself on him. What a skank. I was going to make sure that we all kept in contact and didn't care how much her little friend disliked it. Mecca was a good girl, and she deserved a good guy, and Jay was that guy.

I handed Mecca back her phone as she sipped on her drink with her back to the dance floor. I felt bad for her. I guess she couldn't take another minute of her friend's outright disrespect, but I knew she would never tell her that. That was ok. I was glad I met Mecca tonight. She helped me out, so it was my duty to return the favor. We were going to be good friends and that Sasha girl was going to hate the day she ever laid eyes on me wrong. I looked around to see Jay walking back towards us, but the song wasn't over. I knew it. He was tired of her shit too.

"Man, your friend is crazy." He shook his head at Mecca, reclaiming the stool next to her and rubbing her arm. I saw Miss Thang following, not too far behind him. She looked even crazier.

"Uhhh Mecca, Let's go!"

"Damn Sasha. Why you gotta be all rude and whatnot?" she looked puzzled by her friend's demands.

"I'm not rude honey. We just got stuff to do, and this is a waste of time." Putting her hand on her hip to let her know she meant business.

Mecca hung her head then looked over to Jay and I and apologized, "Hey guys, I'm sorry, but she's my ride."

"I can give you a ride," I offered, intentionally pissing Sasha off. "Hell, Jay can even take you home." I looked over at Jay as he nodded yes.

"Fine! Stay your ass here with strangers then." Sasha twirled around and stomped off like a five-year-old having a temper tantrum.

"Honey, what in the hell is wrong with your *best* friend? Jay and I were both appalled.

"Oh, she's probably just had too much to drink. Can't take her nowhere." She tried to laugh it off.

"I think you should go check on her beautiful." Jay expressed.

"I think I should too. I'll be right back guys. Excuse me." She got up and walked towards the exit.

"Man, that chic needs her ass whipped." I was agitated at this point.

"You don't even know the half, sis. This chic had the audacity to tell me that she and Mecca were taking me home with them for a threesome." I looked disgusted.

"What the fuck? Are you kidding me?"

"No, ma'am. And then, Sasha went on to tell me how she spoke for Mecca and they were a package; if I wanted Mecca, she had to be in the middle."

"Get the fuck outta here man!" I couldn't believe the shit I was hearing.

"Man, it was a turn-off. It made me look at Mecca side-ways for real." He shook his head.

"Nah, that ain't her. From the little bit of time we spent together, I can tell she has a genuine heart and is nothing like Sasha."

"I sure hope not because I was feeling her. It was just something about her that caught my eyes. By the looks of things, I may never find out because I'm sure that she won't be back once she finds her friend." He was disappointed.

"No worries Bro. I gotcha. I put your number in her phone while you were on the dance floor and I dialed my number from her phone to make sure we had a good contact number for her too." I rubbed his back.

He was a good guy and deserved a good woman like Mecca. I was going to make sure that Sasha wouldn't come between the two of them if it were the last thing I did.

Mecca

I felt embarrassed by the way Sasha was acting and treating my new friends. She'd always been a bit jealous, but damn. Deep down inside I understood that she was only trying to look out for me and my feelings, but I was a grown ass woman, and she needed to be checked about her attitude tonight. I couldn't even enjoy myself and get to know Jay better without her hating on me.

The other side of the club was packed, and I prayed I didn't have to go all over to find her because she wasn't at the bar like she'd promised to be. I swear if it wasn't about her, it didn't matter to her. Jay was sweet, and I was glad that Shauna took my phone and exchanged numbers with me. I honestly couldn't say that I would ever see or talk to them again if she hadn't. I just hoped it didn't seem too forward of me to text her or Jay first.

I decided I wouldn't search the club and just ask the security guy if he saw her leave. I was sure he would remember her because they flirted with each other when we first got there.

"Uh, hi!" I approached the cute one.

"He-llo gorgeous!" he attempted to flirt.

"Do you remember the girl I came in with? You know, the one you were flirting with when we first came in?" I politely reminded him so he could get his mind off me.

"Of course I do," he grinned. "Who could forget that red dress and the body that filled it?"

"Cool, did you see where she went?"

"Sure did. Her fine ass left with some lame ass, Tyrese looking dude."

"Wait! What? She left me?"

"Well, she left this club, but not its parking lot!" he laughed.

"What the hell does that mean?" I was frustrated with his antics.

"Damn baby. You're a little slow, aren't you? Your girlfriend is getting freaky in a car that's in this parking lot." He broke it down for me like I was five.

"You don't have to be a smart ass!" I scorned.

"Well, you acting like you don't know your friend is a freak."

"Whatever man! Since you know so much about her whereabouts, can you point out the car that's parked in the parking lot?" I got smart right back.

"Sure can. It's that blue Yukon with rims on the third row." He pointed.

I felt disgusted. Not because Sasha was swinging an episode in the back seat of some stranger's jeep because she didn't have any shame in her game, but because the windows were all fogged up and the damn truck was rocking side to side. I just shook my head and headed to the truck.

I didn't want to interrupt, but I wasn't sure if she was coming back in the club or not and that she didn't want Jay so I could be serious about talking to him. I knew it sounded crazy because I met him first, but I didn't care. In my life, Sasha always came first and according to the rule, if she wanted him, I had to back off. It was just easier that way. I had to make sure nothing or no one came in between my best friend and me ever again. I'd made that mistake before, and it wasn't a good experience for any of us.

Marco was so jealous and possessive when it came to our relationship. He didn't want me to hang out with Sasha or even be around her for real. I messed that up when I tried to be honest with my man. I talked too damn much and messed it up for us. Once he realized Sasha wasn't a one-man-woman, like me; he didn't have it. He called her whores and disrespected her to a point where he made me choose between them both; I chose Sasha.

Other than that, he would have been the perfect guy for me. Sasha always said that if a man displayed that much jealousy in a relationship and judged someone based off of their friends, it would only get worse. I guess I dodged the bullet, but sometimes it still felt crazy. We had so much in common and wanted the same things in life. It's funny how friends can see things that you can't when love blinds you. Thank God for Sasha!

As I approached the truck, I heard moans and groans. It was going to be harder than I thought. The closer I got, I saw Sasha's red stiletto pressed against the window. I thought it over again and asked myself if it was a good idea to interrupt, but gathered myself and got the nerve to knock on the same window.

Knock, knock, knock! I knocked hard three times.

Sasha's shoe disappeared from the window as it rolled down. I heard her say, "Shit! Who the fuck is that?" Then he yelled, "I don't know."

He stuck his head out the window, and before he could say anything to me, Sasha realized it was me and said, "Oh, that's my best friend. You know, the one who reneged on us." My feelings were hurt. She'd been discussing me with some random guy.

He says, "Ohhh! Baby girl, did you change your mind?" with a weird smirk on his face.

"Hell no. How can I change my mind about something I didn't know anything about?" I gave him attitude.

Sasha sucked her teeth, "Well, I guess that's my cue to leave."

"What you mean that's your cue to leave? You didn't do me back as you promised." He was upset.

"Well let's just call it a 68 and I owe you one." She kissed his cheek, slid her dress back down, and hopped out of the truck.

"Oh, hell naw. This is some bullshit." Homeboy didn't want to let it go like that.

"Baby, I promise I will make it up to you later." She seductively ground her ass on his bulging print. "It wasn't enough room for all the things I planned to do you tonight anyway." She stroked his ego.

Dude zipped up his pants with the condom still on; pissed. She couldn't get out of his truck fast enough before he took off screeching tires.

"So you finally decided to come check on me I see?" she eyeballed me with her hand on her hip.

"What do you mean? I left right after you did. Then you weren't where you said you'd be and I had to ask the thirsty security guy where you went." I felt bad for not leaving when she left.

"Soon as I did huh? Okay. I had time to get ole boy, go to his truck, and get some basic ass head, but you were right behind me though?" she spoke sarcastically.

"Listen, Sasha. It's been a long night, and we haven't even been here an hour for real." I was irritated.

"Don't get all cute with me Miss look at me with my new friends."

"I'm not getting cute Sasha. I am grown and thought I could talk to or spend time with who the hell ever I choose." I rolled my neck.

"So you're really gonna choose some nobodies over me?" she played on my emotions by changing her voice.

"No. Of course not, but you didn't have to be like that towards Jay and Shauna. They are cool people."

"Who is cool people? Not that girl and definitely not that lame ass little boy." She started walking towards her car.

"So you have no interest in Jay?" I phished.

"Hell and NO! He's super whack. I just wanted to see where his mind was and just like I thought, it was in the clouds. I thought he could have been our third party for the night, but after talking to him, I think he may be gay. I mean look at what he was wearing! Who where's a suit to The Alley?" she laughed.

"Gay? Really? I didn't get that from him or his sister." I thought hard.

"Of course you didn't, sweetie. Were you expecting him or his sister to tell you he was gay? That's what I'm here for. My Gaydar is always on point." She grabbed the keys out of her purse and hit the alarm twice to unlock the car doors. "So, what happened to our original plan girl?" she stared at me as I snapped my seat belt.

"I guess we can make it happen another night." I felt uneasy.

"You guess? What, you're having second thoughts now?" she pressured.

"No, I didn't change my mind. I just think that after everything that went on tonight, I'm not in the mood to talk about that." I turned my head and faced the window thinking about Jay.

"Woooowwww! I see how it is, best friend. You done let some strangers get all in your damn head and now you want to be a re-nigger." She was pissed.

"Not at all. I just remember what you told me about Marco acting all jealous and stuff, and you kind of reminded me of him a lot tonight." I refused to look her in the eyes.

"Cool. So now you're gonna compare me to Marco's overly jealous ass." She taunted.

"Damned if I do, damned if I don't," I mumbled.

"What you say?"

"Nothing Sasha. Can we stop by a 7-eleven, on the way home, please? I need some double A batteries." I attempted to change the subject.

"Is that what we do now?" I felt her eyes burning the back of my head.

"What?"

"Change the subject like we're the strangers." She insisted I look at her by grabbing my arm.

I snatched away, "Stop Sasha!" I begged.

"Stop Sasha." She repeated, nudging me in my side to make me laugh. "Those batteries and little toys not gonna give you what Carl could have given you."

"Did you ever think that maybe I wasn't interested in what Carl could give me, especially after he gave it to you first?" I surprised myself.

"Well, damn. Tell me how you really feel?" Sasha laughed. "Are you big mad or little mad?"

"I'm not mad at all, just a little tired." I lied.

"So, now we're lying to each other. I see. First, you changed the subject, now you're fucking lying to me?" she balled around a corner.

"What do you want me to say, Sasha? You had your fun so why are you so mad?"

"Mad? Mad? I'm not mad; I'm heated. You are my best friend and all of a sudden you feel the need to fucking lie to my face? That's the reason why I don't like you meeting new people because every single time you do, you change up on me." She started driving crazy.

"I'm sorry Sasha. I didn't change on you. I just don't see the big deal in having other friends besides you. Healthy people have other friends, Sasha." I knew that would set her off, but I was tired of holding my tongue.

"So, now our friendship is unhealthy? You are truly something special; you know that?" She pulled over and flew into the first park she saw.

"Ok, Sasha. Do you want the truth? Here it is. I'm sick of walking in your shadows. Everything is about Sasha and what Sasha wants. I can't have a life without you acting like the world is going to end. I'm tired of feeling like you are my girlfriend instead of my best friend. You can see and fuck whomever, whenever you want, but not me. I have to clear every fucking thing through you like you're my mother or something. I know you want to protect me from heartache and pain, but I think I need to experience life as normal people do. If someone wants to have coffee with me, I'd like to go without feeling guilty or like I'm cheating on you. I shouldn't have to hide anything from you, but the way you act makes me want to hide everything from you. Just like tonight when you just grabbed Jay and took him on the dance floor to try and seduce him. You didn't give a damn if I liked him or he liked me. Sasha always gets first dibs on every man. I'm sick of it. I like Jay and his sister, Shauna. And, I plan on being friends with them if they still want to be friends with me whether you like it or not." I exhaled.

"Okay." That was all she said.

"Okay what? You don't have anything to say?" I was confused.

"Nope." She sat tight-lipped.

"Come on Sasha. Don't be like that. I love you more than I love myself and you're tripping right now."

Sasha refused to say another word, so there was a weird silence in the car as she pulled up to the house. That's right; we lived together too. I knew she was mad, but she'd never given me the silent treatment before. It was awkward as hell. I felt bad, but she needed to hear every word. So, I jumped out of the car and headed towards the door. I listened for her to close her door and come in the house behind me, but she didn't. She pulled off as soon as I opened the door. I closed the door behind me and just stood there and cried.

To Be Continued...

Made in the USA
Columbia, SC
13 March 2025